LOST CHILDREN OF THE VATICAN:

Burning Hell

Helena Paneyko

First printing December 2023

ISBN: 979-8-218-31487-3

DISCLAIMER:
LOST CHILDREN OF THE VATICAN is a work of fiction. Names, characters, businesses, places, events, locales, and incidents are either the products of the author's imagination or used in a fictitious manner. Any resemblance to actual persons, living or dead, or actual events is purely coincidental.

Publisher: The Voice of Spanish
Contact: helenapaneyko@gmail.com

LOST CHILDREN OF THE VATICAN:

Burning Hell

"If this is to end in fire,
then we should all burn together.
Watch the flames burn high into the night."
Ed Sheeran

Table of Contents

DEDICATION

To my family, my friends who I consider my extended family, my teachers and professors, my colleagues and all who have crossed my path.

To all the victims of abuse and to those who are still searching for their true identities and justice, despite attempts to silence them, and to silence the truth about their betrayal by The Church.

ACKNOWLEDGEMENTS

I want to acknowledge and give special thanks to Maryjean Cundiff Boyer, Karli Mueller and Nancy Wall Austin for understanding my message in "my unpolished English" and making it shine. And to Heidi Hansen who put it all together and made this work and dream come true!

SECRETS OF CONFESSION

Teach The Children Well,
Their Father's Hell Will Surely Go By

Cardinal Giuseppe Pannini sat with his back to the wall in a corner of a local coffee shop. He bore no sign of the red cloth associated with his standing in the church. While he waited for his guest, he sipped coffee recalling the events of the evening before with the two altar kids, unsure whether the sudden twisting in his gut was from fear or excitement. They were both sleeping when his hard soled, distinctive footsteps woke the dormitory. GP knew the kids were recent arrivals at the orphanage, and he planned to give them a proper welcome, training, as he called it. Sister Juliana had nudged the two, who rubbed their sleepy eyes, and led them to the cardinal. "Will we get sweets?" the little girl asked her brother as they left the dormitory. He held her hand tightly, quite certain that they would not be receiving candy.

"Children!" exclaimed the cardinal. Dressed in his Holy Vestiges, he towered over the young recruits. "You must help me into my night clothes. It is a holy act." As the children carefully removed and laid aside the cardinal's clothes, GP glanced out the window and saw nothing but black . . .

"GP, Buona Sera!"

Startled from silent recall of last night's training, GP tried to stand but his chair hit the wall. It was impolite not to stand while greeting Father Macias, founder, and head of the respected Christo Education Foundation.

Together, they had started the institute in 1914, and the foundation had been so successful there were now education houses all over the world. GP knew that their shared interest in education, but most of all children, had contributed to their success. That and God's help of course.

"Stay seated cardinal," Father Marcias waved and pulled a chair to sit himself. He leaned across the table and stared directly into the cardinal's eyes. "We are providing education to the poor masses, just as we are commanded. But we can serve more. There are children in Europe, particularly in Ireland, where the ravage of war has separated many families." With eyelids lowered and his mouth a slash, the father leaned in further and spoke softly to GP. "I wonder, my friend, can you help me help these poor children of God find their way to Mexico?"

GP had his marching orders, orders as if given by Pope Benedict XVI himself.

* * *

After planning to travel to Dublin, GP began the process of recruiting students from the local parishes for Father Macias's Education Foundation. Yes, he thought, this is a wonderful opportunity for Father Macias and me. Not only will we be surrounded by young children, but we are doing God's work, helping these children of God to enter his kingdom. No one could possibly question their motives. More likely, families will be busy competing for the opportunity to be true Catholics.

Dressed in all red accoutrements, Cardinal Giuseppe gathered 50 children for the education mission, promising their families the children would have a first class education, full bellies and warm beds. GP then escorted the children directly to Father Macias. Even though the children were afraid and alone, away from their families for the first time and untrusting, they were so very hungry. The nice man in red kept his promise and fed them a big meal that night, including lamb. The children hadn't had meat in ages.

Shortly thereafter, GP joined Macias and a dozen other educators de Christo, to begin the children's formal training.

JOE O'CONNOR

Joe O'Connor, the presiding judge, was known to be incorruptible, as many who had tried to corrupt his rulings had learned the hard way. His decisions were sometimes unpopular and at other times applauded by fellow judges and counselors. Joe O'Connor saw his duty as a purposeful balance of the scales, both the word and spirit of the law. More than anything else though, the judge's thirst for justice drove his decision making. Those who knew him well would say Joe O'Conner was a good listener and a man of faith. He was also a philanthropist who established a foundation called Justice for the Young Angels which supported a Mexican Orphanage, the same orphanage where he had been adopted with his little brother, Javier, by their loving and attentive parents, David and Susan O'Connor.

Joe and Javier attended a private Catholic School and their adopted parents hired tutors to come to their home and help the boys catch up with their classmates. They learned English quickly and excelled in their studies. By graduation, both had earned full scholarships.

José was accepted at Harvard University. He finished his undergraduate studies and stayed in Boston, Massachusetts to attend law school, graduating Summa Cum Laude. Law came easily to José. He breathed in every case study as if it were sea-salted air from his beloved home in Port Townsend, Washington. While he studied law, his brother was accepted into Stanford University's prestigious medical school. Their parents were extremely proud of the two sons they'd raised. and pleased with the kind, nurturing men, they'd become.

Despite long distances and busy schedules, the family stayed close. David and Susan were the boy's parents in every way except biology. As the only parents they'd ever known, even at an early age, the boys understood how fortunate they'd been to have loving parents worthy of respect. David and Susan retired in Port Towsend in a lovely restored Victorian home, nestled against the Pacific Ocean and surrounded by Bald Eagles, massive Fir Trees, and manicured Rhododendron gardens. Joe and Javier routinely came home for Easter, Thanksgiving and Christmas celebrations. When José was feeling pressure from a full docket and he needed to refocus, there was no place better than his parent's home to clear his mind and help him return to balance. For him, Port Townsend was a sanctuary, and the most peaceful place on Earth.

Sitting at his dad's desk, Joe reviewed incoming work emails on his laptop. One email immediately caught his attention; a request to hear another case at the Seattle Courthouse. Reviewing notes about the case in the email, Joe sighed when he realized it was another high profile, high visibility case, this time involving members of the Catholic Church. The case was brought by the Seattle District Attorney, based on allegations by Andreanna Pannini Buerguenthal against a cardinal named Giuseppe Pannini and the cardinal's brother, George Pannini, a bishop. Multiple affidavits and sworn depositions were attached from an investigator for Adreanna and the DA, but nothing was included in the email from the defendants. He swept his wavy dark and silver tinged hair from his forehead and whispered to himself, "Interesting." The lack of documents from defendants could mean many things. It wouldn't be the first time the legal clerks at the courthouse had simply forgotten to attach the entirety of case documents. Then again, there were other times when silence from defendants spoke volumes.

Glancing out the office window, Joe noticed the sun was hanging on the horizon just above the wind swept Pacific Ocean. He needed to take a walk to clear his head and be totally present for dinner with his parents in a couple of hours. He slipped off his shoes and socks, pulled his hoodie on, exited the back door, and strolled down the sandy path which led to the beach.

With cold sand between his toes, Judge O'Conner always stopped to examine shells, sticks, and seaweed oddities the tide had left behind. He considered himself a serious academic and yet, the freedom and wildness of the Washington coastline never failed to ignite his imagination. He imagined a beautiful young woman walking towards him along the beach from the other direction. With his ready smile, chocolate brown eyes, and boyish good looks, he'd engage the beauty in conversation until she accepted an invitation to dinner with his parents. Then he laughed a full throated roar which couldn't be heard over the surf. Wouldn't she be surprised that this dark olive skinned man was an O'Conner.

CARDINAL GIUSEPPE PANNINI

The heavy, quick strides of Cardinal Giuseppe Pannini's footsteps intruded upon the silent, polished, and wide hallways of the Vatican. The cardinal was impossible to ignore. Acting as an alarm of sorts, peers and visitors scurried out of his way and the possibility of verbal fire. He was simply called GP. As one of the future candidates to become the next Pope, he donned the red casquet and red shoes with a pectoral cross lavishly decorated in precious stones hanging on his chest, a symbol of his hierarchy. A message from the concierge just ten minutes before stated that a document had arrived requiring his immediate signature. As he hurried to the concierge's office, a feeling of dread spread from his chest, down his arms to his hands which were quivering of their own volition. GP had an inkling of what this important document might be, and it wouldn't be good news.

The concierge was standing erect as GP entered the office suite. "Where is it?" the cardinal demanded.

"I have it right here, Cardinal Pannini." Obviously nervous, the concierge turned and collected an envelope from his desk, and then promptly dropped it as he attempted to hand the envelope to GP. "So, very sorry, Your Excellency," he stammered as he scooped up the envelope.

Scowling at the skinny concierge, GP growled, "And where might the signature form be? Do you believe you can pass it to me without dropping it on the floor?'

"Of course, of course. I did not expect you to arrive so quickly." The concierge stepped to a closet in the rear of the office and began digging through papers stored there.

"I have important business to attend to. Your disorganization is unacceptable!'

"Here it is!" The concierge shouted, and rapidly scampered with his head lowered to his desk and pulled a pen from a box. "If you will, please, step over here."

By the time the cardinal stooped to sign the paper, his hands were shaking so badly it was almost impossible to sign his name. He scribbled a rough approximation of his signature, gave the concierge one last disgusted look, and all but ran out of the office.

The concierge signed the receipt as well and whispered to himself, "Well that was unpleasant. I wonder what's in that envelope?"

GP's strides grew in length and speed as he returned to his luxurious apartment. He poured himself a straight Scotch, downed it in one swallow, and turned his attention to the sealed envelope. Though nervous, GP was not surprised by its contents. It was a letter *"inviting"* him to a trial where he was the accused. His brother, Bishop George Pannini, was named as co-defendant.

Why had it taken so long, he wondered?

The color drained from the cardinal's face, as he loosened his vestments - as if the mere act of doing so could free him from his tribulations. Andreanna, the Pannini brothers' younger sister, was listed in bold, dark letters, as the accuser.

THE PANNINI FAMILY

Their father, a physician, was one of the most respected and well-known men in Reggio Emilia, a quaint little village in Northern Italy. Their mother stayed at home except for daily visits to the market and, of course, to the church. She attended church daily where she lit candles and prayed the rosary. She was a strong disciplinarian, and showed her love through cookies, as she lacked even the slightest sense of humor.

During the Italian Civil War (1943-1945) the Panninis decided to emigrate to the United States. The three children were all still younger than five years of age when they made the move to America.

REPORTER MAX

On the morning of February 12th, the weather was unsurprisingly cloudy, rainy and a little bit on the cold side, as it was for most of the winter in Seattle. The city had received an unusual amount of snow two weeks before the trial, but the rain had washed it away and it didn't appear weather would slow justice.

Seattle traffic near the courthouse was a nightmare. News of the impending trial and salacious allegations against senior leaders of the Catholic Church had spread like wildfire. Even the national media had taken an interest, and reporters littered the streets and sidewalks around the stately Seattle courthouse. Every seat was taken in the courtroom itself. The attendees were a mixture of lawyers, journalists, policemen, priests, nuns, civilians, parents, a smattering of teenagers, as well as trial witnesses. Unruly reporters still outside the doors of the courtroom clamored to get in, held back only by the diligent efforts of court security guards.

One journalist from the New York Times who went by the name Max, noticed Cardinal Pannini, who rosary in hand, seemed to be asking for God's last minute celestial help. That's rich, Max thought to himself. He glanced in the other direction to Andreanna, the sister of the accused.. She was quite attractive with long red hair and green eyes, dressed in a somber and feminine dark blue suit. Her black high heels and matching leather purse coupled with her demeanor conveyed an unusual level of confidence. Andreanna's obviously supportive husband sat with their son directly behind Andreanna in the gallery.

The prosecutors were an older man, and a younger woman. The Times reporter had read that they'd been preparing for this case for almost two years. The female prosecutor had relayed in an interview that the more evidence they'd gathered, the more passionate they'd become about prosecuting this case. She said, "This trial has evolved into a personal mission for both me and my co-counsel."

Next to their Vatican-appointed council, the Pannini brothers sat erect and stared directly ahead. Except for the sweat on the brow of the cardinal, they appeared like wooden statues. Max wondered if fate had finally caught up with those monsters.

Behind the defense was a group of adults who as children, had been part of the Cathedral's choir at San Luis Potosí, in Mexico, when the cardinal's brother George Pannini had served there as a priest. They were here to act in the capacity of witnesses for the defense.

Max had conducted extensive research into the historical background for this trial. He'd learned that the Metropolitan Cathedral Virgen de Guadalupe was built in 1670 and was in the main plaza of the old city. Located on one side of the cathedral, a Catholic school provided education to many children of the area. The growing population of "Potosinians," mostly Catholics, was comprised of loyal parishioners who would never dream of questioning the authority of any of the priests and nuns who served as teachers. It would most definitely have been considered a sin to do so. Amen.

The extent of the religious complex went beyond the cathedral and the school. An orphanage and a pseudo-convent close by functioned as part of an intertwined and secret plan to control the world.

According to the research, the pseudo-convent was directed by the Opus Dei, an extremist branch of the Catholic Church, capable of brainwashing young girls and making them fanatics and willing slaves to their superiors. There were two categories of girls: The first were upper-class girls from wealthy families who supported religious leaders. This group was very proud of having been selected to be a part of this kind of "Cofradia." And then there were the "rest." These girls came from under-privileged families who believed their girls had been taken away to better their education and social status. Once these children had entered the "convent" and were living inside its walls, none of them would be allowed contact with the outside world, ever again. The first-class girls had special classes including "Understanding of the world according to Josemaría Escrivá," a course on how to engage new generations in their cause. The second-class girls, mostly of indigenous origins, were used as slaves for the other girls, cleaning, cooking, and caring for them. In addition, they had to sexually serve the so called "priests" of the complex, not just to satisfy their appetite, but also to produce babies which were then separated from their mothers and sent to the orphanage. There, these infants were given up, a nice name for sold.

Max was both excited and hesitant to cover the trial. Bi-lingual, he knew that he could more easily interview witnesses who spoke primarily Spanish. He was also raised Catholic and understood the culture. Overall, he was honored to have been asked, but the death of his grandmother, Georgette made the trial far more personal.

As Max waited for the trial to begin, he looked down at the white gold ring on his right hand. The black stone sparkled in the fluorescent lights of the courtroom. Two initials were engraved on the inside: VG. The ring had been given to him as a symbol of life-long dedication, and it became both a special talisman and inspiration to Max. He'd worn the ring everyday since he'd been bequeathed it by his grandmother.

He thought about that spring day, when he and his family were at his beloved grandmother's side while she struggled through her last moments of life. She was ninety-three at the time of her death. Max wondered how she'd made it that long after smoking unfiltered Camel cigarettes like a chimney for most of her life. She'd only quit when she'd received a diagnosis of pulmonary emphysema. Max shook his head remembering how she kept fighting though, dragging that oxygen bottle around with her everywhere, always ready with a quip or a laugh.

Georgette loved purple violets. Even on her last day, her favorite flowers were prominently displayed on a dresser in her room at the assisted living facility. How she'd managed to get them here, or who had brought them for her, Max still didn't know, but he had a good guess.

As he'd moved into her room for what was probably the last time, Max was startled at how frail and colorless his grandmother appeared. Even so, her glasses were as always on top of whatever book she was in the process of reading, frequently a novel written in French. A Rococo lamp, an owl collection, a map of Paris, and a huge assortment of books along one wall adorned her private space.

The door to her closet was open and mostly empty. She'd never been particularly interested in collecting clothing. The garments she did own were all high quality, sophisticated and elegant. She was of a generation and culture where the wearing of pants was considered an offense.

The ring Max was wearing now was kept in a box stored in a mahogany secretary which sat in a far corner of the room, and like pants, he'd never seen his grandmother wear the ring. Maybe that explained why it fit his much larger finger. What she wore was a wedding ring, as was the tradition of her time.

A man Max had never seen before sat in a chair by his grandmother's bedside. The man stood up and walked over to shake hands when Max entered. He'd heard from the nurse taking care of Georgette that there was a man in the room and that he'd been visiting daily. No one ever questioned why he'd been visiting or who he was. His grandmother was known for keeping secrets. She either became angry or brushed off any questions about her past. It was no surprise to Max then that when the man grabbed his hand in a firm grip, he mumbled "I'm Vincente" and spoke a last name that was unintelligible. One thing was certain; he may have been the same age as Georgette, but he was in far better condition.

Max vividly remembered watching as his grandmother left this world. It was significant because it was the first time a close relative or friend had passed. While his mom and aunts cried, Vincente maintained a stoic countenance. It was as if the group gathered was inhaling in unison, willing Georgette to continue breathing. Suddenly her eyes came open, she smiled, stared at Vicente one last time, and serenely drifted off into the universe, finally at peace.

It was interesting to Max that his grandmother had refused confession and last rites before passing. He'd heard from his mom there were many good reasons for her choice. Georgette's life had been filled with hardship and horror as a direct result of the religion her parents had forced upon her. Max had once overheard his grandmother say that the Catholic religion fell far short of following its own principle of "Love thy neighbor."

After Georgette's last moments, Vincente got up and bolted out the door, leaving Max's family to cry and tell stories about their grandmother. An hour later, they began the emotionally difficult task of cleaning, sorting, and boxing her personal effects.

Among other things, an unusual wooden box filled with papers was sitting on the top shelf of her closet. Some of the papers were so old they'd yellowed along the edges. Max's sister, Gabi had gently lifted the papers from the box and set the pile on the small table in their grandmother's suite. As she thumbed through some of the documents that were mostly written in their grandmother's hand, Gabi gasped aloud. "You're not going to believe this, Max. These papers are in chronological order. This is a written account of grandma's life, like her own autobiography. All the things that she would never share."

Max grabbed the top bundle held together by a large paperclip. He studied the first page, and at the very top of the page in his grandmother handwriting she wrote, "What I desire most is for the truth to become known. I have carried that burden for most of my life, and as death chases me, I find I need to kill that beast to finally have peace."

"I wonder what truth she was talking about?" Max whispered to his sister.

Max looked up when the noise in the courtroom increased. The judge's door was opening. Max had been working on the transcription of his grandmother's autobiography and was almost done. More than anything, he hoped this trial might tie up some loose ends before he published a novel about his grandmother's life.

"ALL RISE!"

The Presiding Judge, Joe O'Connor, entered the courtroom.

OLYMPIA, WA

The Presiding Judge, Judge Susan Stonemaker, was also about to enter the courtroom in another important case involving Catholic leaders. The defendant, Bishop George Pannini, Giuseppe Pannini's brother, was the same George Pannini currently on trial with his brother in Seattle. Since George couldn't be in two places at once, his legal defense representative sat in for him. Appointed by the Vatican due to his experience in trials of this sensitive nature, Conrad Jacobson had two responsibilities: to sit in the defendants chair and act as George's lawyer in the case. He'd pleaded with George to ask for a continuance because all accused are allowed to face their accusers, but George stated simply, "I would prefer not to be there anyway."

ADRIAN DELOUVRIER

Adrian Delouvrier, the last surviving adopted son of Georgette, helped to bring the prosecution of George's crimes, based largely on evidence he'd gathered from his deceased brother Ricardo. The case involved an alarming number of children with disabilities in Palmiras del Picacho, a few kilometers south of San Miguel de Allende. They were allegedly entirely George Pannini's victims. Before George had taken on the assignment in Palmiras, the number of cases of children with problems had never been unusually high, but that had changed drastically during the time that he was there. Father Pannini also travelled to San Miguel de Allende quite frequently where he acted as the Director of the Children's Choir at the main Cathedral. His brother happened to be the Chaplain there at the time.

Thanks to advances in genetic science, and since they shared a resemblance, Ricardo and Adrian, known as Georgette's adopted sons, had been able to verify their heritage. They discovered they were indeed both sons of the same father, Max's grandfather Antoine. The genetics also showed that Adrian was not an adopted son at all, but rather Georgette's biological child, while Ricardo's mother was a nun with the monastic name of Sor Alegría. They were half-brothers all along.

Sor Alegria had fallen madly in love with Antoine. The story the brothers had learned was that Sor Alegría left the church after Ricardo was taken from her, but she'd been subjected to torture and punishment inconceivable in a religious environment before she could escape. Her dreams of leaving that evil place were thwarted again and again. She was under strict surveillance, often locked up in her bedroom, isolated from everyone and everything. Once, she even attempted suicide but they found her before the rope strangled her. She was forced to fast for days on end to break her spirit, but she remained unbroken.

Sor Algeria finally succeeded in escaping through a bathroom window. No one ever learned where she went. The only way Ricardo had confirmed she was his mother was DNA hair left on brush before she escaped. At the convent word spread that she'd passed away. There was even a tombstone with her name placed in the cemetery.

Years later out of the blue, Sor Alegría arrived at Max's grandmother's house. She'd knocked, and

Ricardo, who happened to be visiting at the time, opened it. As soon as she saw him she recognized her blood, even though she'd never been allowed to hold him in her arms. The frail woman was so overwhelmed that she fainted. Ricardo was able to catch her before she hit the ground. As soon as he held her in his arms, he felt shivers up his back. In that instant, a family had finally found each other. When Sor Algeria recovered from her fainting spell, mother and son cried their bittersweet tears as one. Ricardo felt a fierce sense of protectiveness for his mother. She was delicate, and exhausted from her lifelong travails.

RICARDO

Ricardo had become a doctor and devoted himself to pediatrics because of a special gift for children. When they arrived at his office, children were relaxed and even happy, instead of displaying the more common panic that usually afflicts younger patients. Ricardo also had a very special sense of humor. At work, he wore a red ball on his nose that the children could squeeze. When they did, it sounded like a frog croaking during a full moon. The sound, however, was actually being made by Ricardo himself. Along the way he'd picked up the skills of a ventriloquist, which is how he answered any questions the little children asked. They, in turn, never really knew where the answers were coming from. They looked for the source of the voice behind the desk, the stretcher, or the curtains. Ricardo became one of the most beloved and respected pediatricians in his city. In addition to being an extraordinary pediatrician, he was known as a brilliant man and quite charitable.

During a rural medical internship, Ricardo found he enjoyed small town life and remained in the area during his professional years. There he met the love of his life Clara Elena, with whom he had two children, Luis Eduardo and Juan Andrés.

A stream of crystal-clear water ran through the town he and his family lived in. During the wet season the stream rose without overflowing and during the dry season, the stream had enough water to enjoy swimming and fishing. The townsfolk were like a big family and treated each other accordingly. The houses still had their porches out front and neighbors would greet each other and visit as someone walked down the main street.

His family was happy in the small town so he stayed. Additionally, Ricardo felt he was needed in the area. He'd noticed an unusually high number of children with intellectual disabilities or certain genetic problems in comparison to the rest of the country. People with disabilities were hidden at home and the doctor was called for private consultations only. His scientific curiosity made him pay closer attention to the issue. He ruled out malnutrition, parental age, infectious diseases and since the town had no industry, he wasn't concerned with chemical pollutants. Finally, Ricardo invited a colleague to undertake a genetic study of the affected children. The results were nothing short of astonishing.

The mothers and fathers of these disabled children were most often half-siblings, and they shared the same father, the parish priest at the time, George Pannini. The DNA results were undeniable. Not only did the parents of the disabled children have the same father, but the three nuns assigned to the parish had been the mothers of these children. They learned the nuns had been repeatedly raped, but they'd never dared to speak up.

The silence was finally broken. It was a major scandal at the time. Not long after the news leaked out, Ricardo was found dead in the woods with knife wounds in his back. His colleague, who had helped with the genetic study, was also murdered. An assassin later confessed to killing both men having been hired by the priest who'd been the father of the children.

The priest was never brought to justice and the case was permanently shelved at Apostolic Nunciature. Rather than take appropriate action, the church simply relocated the guilty priest. That was and still is the way the Church deals with such situations.

ADRIAN

Adrian shared something special with Ricardo: an ear for music and sound. Ricardo and Adrian had both been part an all-male chorus of deep voices that sang at the school choir and the church. They sang like angels. In fact, each one of them, due to their special vocal tones, had performed several times as soloists. At home, the brothers listened to classical music extensively.

One of the traditions of the family, in addition to choir membership, was that each child was expected to select and learn a musical instrument. Adrian chose the violin. He was fascinated by the classical composers. Among his favorites were Antonín Leopold Dvořák, Mozart, Vivaldi, Chopin, Bach, Beethoven, and Pyotr Ilyich Tchaikovsky. He practiced every day, for hours at a time and truly enjoyed it. Ricardo could often guess Adrian's mood based on what he was playing.

Adrian chose to devote his professional life to music and singing. He went to the conservatory and, on his own merits, won a scholarship to further his education. His father, of course, thought that being a musician was not a respectable profession and forced him out of the family home. Georgette felt differently about her musical artist son and always supported him, remaining in touch, helping him with money when he needed it, and encouraging him to follow his own path.

When Adrian attended elementary school at San Miguel de Allende, he was forced to use his right hand although he was left-handed by nature. This was mandated by the "dictatorship" of the moment. All children had been forced to become ambidextrous. His father faithfully followed the "regime's" mandate. Instead of leading to intellectual achievement, this practice led to worse outcomes in mathematics, logical reasoning, and even memory issues. Adrian, who was clearly quite intelligent, was labeled unfit for schooling.

At first he also had trouble with the violin. This partly had to do with the fact that there was no such thing as a violin for left-handed musicians at the time. Learning to play the violin was an incredible challenge for him, but he liked it so much that he persevered until he succeeded. He also learned how to play other string instruments.

In time, he became a composer and wrote pieces he played with the symphonic orchestra. Adrian won several international musical prizes and became a well-known musician and composer. He was an excellent example for others facing similar difficulties.

The trial was a landmark moment for Adrian. It was time to act for himself and his deceased brother to set the record straight. It was the best way he knew to do the right thing and honor Ricardo. By demanding the truth, Adrian could finally see justice.

The jury was comprised of nine people who would hear all the statements from the prosecution as well as any affirmative defense the Vatican lawyer conjured up for the defendant. An expert witness and geneticist, specializing in DNA comparisons would also be testifying.

A MARRIAGE OF CONVENIENCE

Georgette finished her studies in Paris. Her marriage had been arranged before she finished school. A military gentleman, a friend of her brother and the son of her parent's friends had been chosen. She'd never even seen her selected fiancé. Unsurprisingly, the wedding was joyless and felt more like a funeral. The newlyweds knew it was a marriage of convenience to keep appearances, even though, in time, husband and wife learned to bear the burden of marriage by raising the children they had procreated plus some "others."

Antoine Louvrier, who was already a lieutenant colonel, was assigned as military attaché to French embassies in several countries in Latin America. The family moved frequently and finally settled down for good in Mexico where most of the children grew up. Georgette oversaw all the activities at home, while Antoine controlled the finances. It was customary to have people helping with the chores at home. There were nannies, cooks, cleaning personnel, gardeners, and a chauffeur at Georgette's disposal. She was not allowed to drive, nor did she know how.

ANTOINE

Antoine was a very conservative man who obsessively went to church on Sundays and holidays, even when ill. Originally, he encouraged Georgette to go along and, in time, also brought along the children: Benjamín, Josephine, Lucía, Verónica, Mónica, Victoria, Adrian, Ricardo, Rosa, and Cristina. The children were born one after another, several even born the same year. Verónica and Mónica, were identical twins.

The first three children, Benjamín, Josephine, and Lucía were Georgette and Antoine's biological children. The others began arriving by the work and grace of their affiliation with the Church, the Holy Spirit, and other collaborators. While very different physically, all the children were welcome, loved, and treated equally regardless of the origin of their birth.

The family had so many children, Antoine and Georgette bought fabric by the roll at good prices through the military commissary to dress them all. An excellent seamstress, Georgette's mother along with a hired sewing assistance made clothes for the children in the same colors. People could easily recognize the family when they were out in the town or at church.

Antoine carefully crafted an image of a kind and dedicated family man, visiting church regularly and confessing at least once a week, but the reality of the man was far from his image. He was in fact a philanderer who took advantage of the power of his military rank to get his way. Once Giuseppe Pannini, the local priest, learned of Antoine's infidelities during supposedly secret confessions, he used that information to blackmail Antoine. The magnitude of Antoine's sins and infidelities were so great that he was forced to accept children in adoption, some of half-unknown origin, to keep the priest's mouth shut.

Blackmail and threats were nothing new in the church. Antoine begrudging accepted the blackmail and paid up by accepting children, while the church continued to emphasize Christian values during services and religion classes.

During this time, it was common for babies to be given, or if possible sold, to new parents in pseudo-adoptions. These adoptions were completed without adoption paperwork. As soon as the infants were born in clandestine clinics, they were given to their new guardians, and the papers showed a legal birth rather than an adoption by using the family name of adopting parents. It appeared to anyone investigating that the children were born to the parents and not adopted. Georgette and Antoine's children were assumed to be birthed by Georgette even though some of their birth dates were only months apart. No one ever dared to ask questions about this unusual coincidence. Many parishioners of the local church were enablers of this practice.

The delivery process for these "orphans at birth" was somewhat more complicated because none of these children were truly orphans. They were the children of religious leaders and their collaborators. Priests, nuns, and people outside the clergy associated with nuns and priests were the parents. Nuns concealed their pregnancies beneath habits and left the convent by means of special permits a few months before childbirth, to arrive at clinics with peculiar arrangements. Staff at these special clinics were required to sign an oath of silence. Any violation of the oath resulted in death by execution, and the bodies of those executed would vanish as if by magic. In the case of sex slaves, many of them decided to leave the cloth and return to civilian life, which of course was nothing short of a treacherous journey. Other women, mostly victimized by priests, were also sent to these clinics to later be exiled to where they would never be found.

ANDREANNA PANNINI BUERGUENTHAL

Andreanna sat tall and unwaveringly behind the prosecutions bench, as the trial against her two brothers, Giuseppe and George, was about to begin. She hadn't seen or spoken to her brothers in decades. She looked down at her sweaty palms, rubbed them together and then gave a defiant scowl directed to her brothers. It made her feel a little more in control to give them a look, even though the dread was still lodged in her stomach. There was no way she'd allow those two disgusting pigs to see her fear. Instead she reached into her purse, pulled out a pen and began taking notes on a legal pad her lawyer had given her.

This was the moment she'd been waiting and preparing for through most of her life. As soon as she heard the Pannini brothers had moved to positions in the U.S Catholic Church, Andreanna knew the time had come. God had sent them here. The secrets she'd had to live with, like a constant weight on her soul, could finally be told, and her brothers would be made to pay. All the world would see the barbarity of what had happened to her. Sometimes the wait for this day seemed like a forever extended, uncomfortable and painful pregnancy. Her husband, Franz Buerguenthal, a former Catholic priest, and their children had given her all the strength and support she needed to make this day happen.

THE PANNINI BROTHERS

The two brothers were their religious mother's dream children. This became even more the case when the brothers decided to attend the seminary and become priests. They were experts at manipulating people for their own benefit.

One morning, while their mother was at church and their father was not around, Giuseppe and George savagely raped their own sister. The brothers took turns holding Andreanna down. They also threatened her with more punishment if she told anyone what had happened. Andreanna was only thirteen years old and a virgin. With this rape, her brothers had taken both her virginity and her dignity.

Andreanna was humiliated and terribly afraid to tell anyone. She feared her brothers would kill her. Three months after the brutal attack, Andreanna started feeling sick and a doctor was called. Her worst fears had been confirmed—she was pregnant. A family friend who'd been visiting for a few days around the time of the occurrence, was conveniently blamed for the rape. His remains were found many years later in a small cemetery by the Basilica di San Prospero.

To avoid scandals, Adreanna was sent to a convent where she gave birth to a son. She was never allowed to see or hold him. The child, Manuel, son to one of her two brothers was taken to an orphanage for disabled children. Andreanna stayed secluded until she was able to escape from her prison. She been forced to pay for a sin she never committed.

Later, Andreanna moved to United States where she became a citizen and a lawyer. As soon as she'd saved enough money, she hired a well-known and capable private investigator named Diego Ramírez, her grandson, and the son of Victoria, one of Georgette's daughters. He would be one of the witnesses at the trial. Diego had collected a literal treasure trove of information on the Pannini brothers, and his exhibits and evidence were all in the custody of Judge O'Connor.

Andreanna's son, Manuel, had been found in one of the church's orphanages. Even though he'd grown up with special privileges because of his relationship to George Pannini, Manuel was disabled and had spent his life in a wheelchair. He also had difficulty with verbal communication.

Diego had obtained a DNA sample from both Manuel and George Pannini.

SOR CARMEN/VICTORIA

Diego's mother, Victoria had been a kind young woman, but she'd lived a very difficult life as an adult. From an early age she'd expressed a desire to become a nun.

When she was 16, her hormones had taken over her nature and sent her on a detour. She fell madly in love with a young man she met while working at a restaurant. Carlos Arias also fell in love with Victoria. He asked Victoria's parents for her hand in marriage, in the old-fashioned way. No expense was spared at their wedding. Javier and Victoria looked like true lovebirds, the perfect couple.

After the birth of six children, Carlos began drinking frequently and heavily. He would return home late each night and scream that his problems were all Victoria's fault. Almost daily, insults and beatings were part of the house routine. While the children pretended to sleep, Victoria was the victim of an abuse that she kept concealed.

When she could take it no longer, Victoria asked Carlos to leave. The children, some of whom were teenagers by then, supported her. Reluctantly, he left.

Carlos used to say that the words "always and never" did not stand for absolutes, and as it turned out in the end, he was right. After many years of living on the streets as a vagrant, he returned to the family home, this time to bid farewell during what would turn out to be the last week of his life. He knew he knocked on Victoria's door that didn't have long because his liver was failing. He returned remorseful, asking for forgiveness. Their children were already grown when he passed.

His death helped Victoria to make the most important decision of her life. As she was now a widow, she was finally able to return to her original idea of becoming a nun and could devote herself to a religious life. From now on, faith, chastity, and poverty would be her vows.

It was difficult for Victoria to find a convent willing to accept her because she was not a virgin, and she was considered impure. Finally, and quite unexpectedly, a letter arrived from a convent willing to accept her. The first five years were to be a trial period after which she would be given the opportunity to finally take her vows. She shared the rest of her life in a congregation whose mission it was to help recovering drug addicts. The nuns essentially lived in absolute poverty. The community helped them with food and clothing, but they lived in an ill-kept convent where rats and spiders were regular guests. The nuns earned no salaries.

The male priests enjoyed some financial privileges due to certain arrangements with their superiors. The priests also received health insurance and the nuns did not. The group of nuns Victoria lived with were educated indigents giving their lives to serve others. In some ways, these nuns could have been considered slaves of religion. With little support from the church but a strong vocation to serve, they helped and assisted everyone they could. Victoria died a happy woman as Sor Carmen. She was buried in simplicity, as she had requested.

The story did not end there…

Diego attended his mother's funeral with his brothers and sisters at a private cemetery. Perhaps because of his investigators eye, Diego felt there was something off about the cemetery where is mother was to be buried. When he began his investigation for Adrianna, he learned quickly that many of the young women and children who'd been abused by the church seemed to disappear. He'd originally thought that they'd escaped, but as the investigation moved along he became convinced that they'd been eliminated by the church. He was talking to Adreanna about the strange graveyard where his mother was buried, when it occurred to him why it might have felt so strange.

After obtaining a special permit from the Department of Justice to investigate the necropolis, a team with penetrating radar was hired to search the grounds for remains. Withing two days the team found evidence of bodies buried where no graves were marked. Digging crews moved in to finish the task, finding eighteen bodies. Based on the size of the skeletons, most appeared to be women. The remains were then sent for corresponding forensic studies, and it was learned that some of the remains matched with nuns reported missing by their families. The one thing they all had in common was a bullet hole in their heads, and records indicating they'd been pregnant and were sent to clinics to have their children.

In another section of the private cemetery, the digging crew also found the remains of several newborn children. Interestingly, at about the same time, a similar scandal became public in Europe.

Diego received threats from "anonymous" sources after the cemetery discovery. It seemed obvious to Diego who might have been responsible for both the threats and the crimes he had unearthed.

LUCÍA

Lucía was Georgette's favorite child. This may have been because Lucía had been a premature baby who barely survived, or maybe, because she was the youngest of Georgette's biological children. More likely though, Lucia felt guilty about not having dedicated enough time to cuddle and share special moments with this child when necessary. Nevertheless, there was a special bond between them.

When Lucía attended high school, she attended a presentation on the missions which made a huge impression on her, probably because she was very sensitive and a fanatic when it came to the Catholic religion. The recruiters were looking for people just like her. She decided not to discuss the topic with her parents. The day came when the missionaries were to depart. Lucía wrote her parents, Georgette and Antoine, a long letter justifying her choice to join the missionaries and asking them to respect the space she was creating for herself.

The group of recruits was sent to a camp, much like a concentration camp, where they were victims of a well-planned brainwashing scheme. They received daily lessons about good and bad, and righteous punishment was always emphasized. This first part of the missionary process was quite difficult even for the very devoted recruits. After a few months, they were taken to a new location.

The new location housed many indigenous children who had been taken, or better said, kidnapped from their homes with the objective of teaching them about catechism and of erasing any last trace of their own culture. These children were not allowed to speak in their mother tongue, and if they were caught doing so, they were severely punished. They were trained to serve as slaves to the most powerful priests who requested their special services.

When Lucía and her friend Oliver finally realized their missionary work was in truth a nefarious scheme by the church, they decided to escape. They walked for many days through the forest. They were confronted by mosquitoes, snakes, spiders, and other dangerous creatures as well as rain and high humidity. When they finally arrived in a more civilized town, they were able to denounce what they had been part of and had witnessed.

No one believed them except for Georgette. A few months later Lucía and Georgette were finally reunited. Lucía had come home.

THE NIGHTINGALE

In a box guarded by two pieces of scented rose paper Max had found the ring he always wore and a note from Georgette that read: "I see much of myself in you. I live my life as though they were two. The external one, the one that can be seen, and the internal one... like that of the nightingale. By the time you find my diary, I will no longer be afraid to let everything show, to let the truth fly... I lost so many years hiding my secrets, protecting them... and for what? I guess so that I could leave my testimony in the end. You are a reporter, Max. Do what needs to be done to make sure the world knows of the horrors the Catholic Church inflicted on their loyal followers."

THOU SHALT LOVE GOD ABOVE ALL ELSE

Isabelita departed for the convent out of conviction despite desperate pleas from her parents and siblings. She had decided to follow her vocation and no one could dissuade her.

Years passed before she took her final vows. The religious ceremony was modest and her whole family attended. To her family, the vows represented a marriage to the Creator.

Isabelita was assigned as a teacher in a school for girls. She was always positive and smiling, and her students loved her. Because the students held Isabelita in such high regard, they also confided in her. Little by little, Isabelita discovered things that she could not reveal, at least not right away.

The school had a perfect manipulator, a chaplain who was also a licensed psychologist. Nothing could be more dangerous to elementary and high school girls than a sick man with those qualifications.

It was mandatory to confess to Father Gustavo, who had just been "relocated" from the Maritsa's School in Barcelona. When the girls confessed, he asked them their names, which he entered into a little notebook. He made the girls believe that their sins were so grave that it was essential for them to follow the assigned penance to receive forgiveness. He appealed to the sixth commandment: "Thou shalt not commit impure acts".

Next, he would call them one by one to his office with the excuse of discussing incidents of improper behavior. Once they reached his office, he would lock the door. The office was dark. Its walls were decorated with a crucifix, a rosary, a picture of the Pope at the time, and a poster with the Ten Commandments of the Catholic Church. There was also a sturdy wooden desk. A microphone that communicated with classrooms using loudspeakers sat on the top of the desk, and behind the desk was a chair made of the same wood. A black sofa completed the decor.

The girls arrived at the office already terrified. Father Gustavo proceeded to threaten that he would lash out at their families if they spoke to anyone about what happened during their encounters. He hypnotized some girls, had others drink the "juice of the Holy Ghost," and the remainder were raped. After the abuse session, he would then send them back to their classrooms. These practices were frequent. When their names were called on the loudspeakers, the girls panicked and tried mightily to conceal their fear.

Isabelita began to note the changes in student grades as well as the loss of interest in classroom work. Worried, she asked the girls leading and nuanced questions in private sessions. She never doubted their stories and as a result, whenever a girl was called to the psychologist's office, she'd follow them and listen at the door.

She also inquired about the origins of Father Gustavo, and learned he'd been relocated after accusations of pedophilia, along with several other priests. He'd been part of a silent trial which became a major scandal due to the number of children abused. These incidents were settled with Vatican money and the promise that the priests involved would be removed from the congregations. The Church, however, never followed through on that part of the agreement, and the scoundrels in question were simply relocated to third world countries, particularly in Latin America. There, they continued their despicable practices, leaving behind a trail of victims, pain, suicides, mysterious disappearances, and ruined lives.

Isabelita documented the girl's testimonies in a notebook she kept under her mattress. She shared her knowledge with her cellmate, another beloved nun, and prayed nightly for God to show her a path and give her the strength to come forward to expose this evil. She had no doubts about the monster nearby.

THOU SHALT NOT KILL

Isabelita couldn't live with herself anymore knowing she was hiding the abuse of children, and went to see the Mother Superior.

A few days after that meeting, Isabelita's body was found on the banks of the Arauca River. She had been raped and strangled, and the notebook under her mattress had disappeared. On her deathbed, the nun sharing Isabelita's room during that time had to clear her conscience, and she revealed what she knew.

Father Gustavo remained a chaplain, not only for the school, but also for the Police and the Army.

Word reached Andreanna's investigation team about Isabelita's death, and several connected experts were paid to clarify the circumstances of Isabelita's murder. One of these experts found a recording that Isabelita's nun friend had left with one of the few people she could talk to and trust. The names of some of the girls, now women, came to light. Cautiously, since none of the victims wanted to share their stories before a priest or the authorities that supported Father Gustavo, the victims shared their stories from their position as protected witnesses, thus overcoming years of silence and fear.

The news found its way to the media and a number of major court trials were opened, not only against Father Gustavo, but also against the Mother Superior and the Catholic Church.

CHRISTMAS

Christmas holidays were very special at Georgette's and Antoine's home. The large family gathered on Christmas morning and exchanged gifts in a unique way. Each family member would only give one gift to one other randomly selected relative. There were three rules for the gift exchange: first, assignments would be kept secret until the actual gift exchange, second, the gift had to be made by the giver and, third, it had to be of special significance to the recipient. This entailed finding out more about the recipient's life. The family tradition carried on even after Isabelita's passing.

Adrian, the musician, was the master of ceremonies, and he wrote a new piece of music each year for the occasion. Everyone gathered and sat in the inner courtyard to listen. The colonial-style house was roomy and in addition to the immediate family, there were often grandchildren, great grandchildren, and family friends.

After the music session, Adrian continued with the blessing and expressed his gratitude for the chance to have the family together once again. He brought a bag with each name written on a piece of paper and drew a name. The named person talked about what he or she had learned about the relative receiving the gift and then handed over the gift, explaining how and why that gift was chosen and what it meant. Then the next person took a turn. While the family members were giving their answers, hot chocolate, nougat, and Panettone was served. A buffet lunch was served immediately after the family testimonials. It was always a very emotional day.

Georgette spent a good part of the year making little gifts for everyone. One year, she spent many hours gathering pebbles whenever she went to the beach. After washing, drying, and painting the stones, she wrote a personal message and then wrapped them in brown paper, and attached a little flower to the package. The messages were relevant to each member of the family. If someone was having a difficult time, the message might read "HOPE." Another year she gave out small plants that she'd grown herself. Everyone received a different plant in a hand-painted pot. The gift also included a little bag filled with mixed seeds and a card with a message. The message said, "Like the seeds, we are all different. We were all planted and had to be patient to germinate. Everyone grows differently with different gifts, your paths marked by uncertain destiny. Some of our seeds will turn into flowers, some into vegetables, and others into medicinal herbs. Please keep this plant and help it grow." That was the last Christmas that Georgette would attend because of failing health.

MISS MENDIZABAL

The Miss, as she was affectionately called, was a third grade teacher. Originally from the Basque country, she was always full of energy and loved teaching. Almost all of Georgette and Antoine's children had been her students, as were their grandchildren.

One day, in biology class, the teacher had devoted time to new scientific advances, such as DNA testing technology which would allow people to know their true family origins. That discussion energized Max and remained imprinted in his mind until sites like Ancestry.com and National Geographic made DNA testing easy. He was quite surprised to learn that Miss Mendizabal was listed in his DNA matches as his likely grandmother. The teacher had obviously sent in her DNA too before her death.

Although Antoine was not in the Ancestry database, Max obtained his grandfather's DNA from Diego and sent the results to a lab. Antoine was in fact Max's grandfather and obviously, he'd had one of his many affairs with the teacher. The Miss always knew. Perhaps that was why she brought up the subject in class and later sent in her DNA—so that everyone else would know too.

VICENTE

Vicente became a very special person in Max's life after he read his grandmother's letters and her journal account of her life. Max would even say if asked, that Vincente was one of his heros. He searched for the strange man who'd attended Georgette's last breath after he learned the importance of Vincente in her life. They met in person. Max found Vicente to be an extremely intelligent and interesting man. Somehow, he and Georgette had managed to keep their unwavering love secret. What Max learned from his grandmother's letters was that even though she'd endured a hard life, Vincente had loyally encouraged her and given her hope. Vincente was supportive of women in an age where that sort of attitude was unusual. Max thought that Vincente proved that it was possible even in male dominated religions and cultures, for there to be good and decent men. It was such a contrast to some men in his family and church, and the knowledge of Vincente restored his faith.

Around 1939, France began recruiting young men to build an armed forces. A war was coming and the French needed to be able to defend themselves against the Nazi's. Vicente was a pacifist, so he decided to desert. Before he left, his mother confessed something to him she had not had the courage to say earlier. Vicente was the son of one of the town's priests. With his mother's revelations fresh in his mind and the conflict approaching, he put on a backpack and with the little money he carried in his pockets, crossed the Pyrenees to reach Spain's Basque country. There he rented a modest room, found a job loading wagons and spent what little he had left over on Spanish lessons. His Spanish instructor's neighbor, a beautiful redhead, became his best friend. He'd practice Spanish with her while she learned French from him. She knew about Vincent's love for Georgette and was very patient with her role in Vicente's life. In the end, they were married, and had one child, Pierre. Vicente became a widower when Pierre was very young, and fully devoted himself to his son.

Before his death, Vicente gave Max some notebooks that he'd kept throughout the years. Vincente obviously possessed artistic talent which was evident in his drawings. Most of Vincent's diaries were just that, a collection of meticulously made ink vignettes--an overview of his life. There were many drawings of Georgette, but towards the end of his notebooks his life with his wife and Pierre dominated. Interspersed were realistic drawings of how he imagined Georgette might look as she aged. He'd never completely let go of her.

After the trial, Max organized an exhibition with Vicente's drawings as homage to Georgette, his grandmother, and Vincente for a great love that had never ended.

When Max heard the verdict of Giuseppe in Seattle, he touched the ring on his finger with the initials "VG" inside, and smiled from deep down inside.

THE VERDICTS

News of the Washington State trials was extensive. As the days progressed and more witnesses took the stand, the salacious allegations against priests and the deeds of the Catholic Church encouraged loud calls for justice from the public.

In the Seattle trial, the judge had confirmed the DNA samples provided by Diego, and taken from the accusers, the defendants, and Manuel. The results showed that Manuel was in fact Cardinal Giuseppe's and Adreanna's son. Given the other supporting evidence from witnesses, the judge pronounced Guiseppe and George guilty of first degree rape of a minor and sentenced them to thirty years for that felony. For the now elderly Guiseppe and George, thirty years was a death sentence. The brothers were immediately handcuffed and led out of the courtroom. A loud cheer erupted from the trial attendees. Judge O'Conner pounded his gavel platform and shouted, "Silence in the courtroom."

What the audience didn't see was Guiseppe falling to his knees outside the door. Reporters caught photos of the incident however, and the next mornings' headlines read, "Pedophile Priests Sentenced to 30 years—One Dies from Heart Attack."

In the Olympia trial, the decision was quite a bit more unexpected. The judge, the Honorable Susan Stonemaker, presented her decision to the court.

"Before I read the jury's verdict, I'd like to begin with a strong recommendation for the Vatican if the Catholic Church and its hierarchy would like to restore trust with its followers. I recommend the Vatican establish a DNA bank for all Catholic Church leaders worldwide. This database would include priests, nuns, and teachers at Catholic schools. I want to be clear that as an American judge, I have no authority to order the church to take any such an action, however, given the prevalence and seriousness of the crimes presented to this court, I believe that approach to be essential." The judge then handed the verdict from the jury to the Bailiff to read.

The jury found George guilty of a long list of serious felonies, from rape, to conspiracy, to murder. He received three life sentences.

THE CONTINUANCE

Dr. Javier O'Connor, brother of Judge, Joe O'Connor, was a scientist. And, as most scientists, Javier was a curious man. He asked his brother to do a DNA sample after the trial so that he could compare his brother's DNA with the Pannini brothers. Javier also sent along a sample of his own DNA. The results came back with a 99.8% match. Both brothers were Cardinal Giuseppe Pannini's biological sons. Judge Joe O'Conner's wasn't astonished to learn that he and his adoptive brother were full-fledged brothers. In many ways they were similar in looks and attitudes. Joe begged Javier to keep the information secret. If it were to get out, Joe might be accused of bias and his rulings could be thrown out. Even though keeping a secret pact went against the judge's ethics and love of the law, the victims of the Pannini brothers deserved justice. A new trial might deny them that, and besides, the cardinal was dead and George had pancreatic cancer--he wouldn't be around for long.

The O'Connor brothers clandestinely travelled to Mexico to locate their biological mother. After a month of searching, they found her living in severe poverty. She was old, sick, and had little to eat. Joe and Javier, together ensured she would never be alone or in need of anything again. When she died, the words on her gravestone read: "To our mother who gave her soul to the world. May she rest in peace."

THE END

The Prayer of St. Francis, Patron Saint of Animals and Veterinarians.

Lord, make me an instrument of your peace.
    Where there is hatred, let me sow love;
    where there is injury, pardon;
    where there is doubt, faith;
    where there is despair, hope;
    where there is darkness, light;
    and where there is sadness, joy.
Oh, Divine Master,
    grant that I may not so much seek
    to be consoled as to console;
    to be understood as to understand;
    to be loved as to love.
    For it is in giving that we receive;
    it is in pardoning that we are pardoned.
    and it is in dying that we are born to eternal life.

BIBLIOGRAPHY

- https://www.futurechurch.org/historia-del-celibato
- https://www.theguardian.com/world/2011/may/25/nazis-escaped-on-red-cross-documents
- https://es.wikipedia.org/wiki/Instituto_para_las_Obras_de_Religi%C3%B3n
- http://puertoreal.cnt.es/denuncias-sociales/658-mas-de-300000-bebes-fueron-vendidos-durante-50-anos-por-la-iglesia-catolica.html
- https://www.elhistoriador.com.ar/que-fueron-las-cruzadas/
- https://es.wikipedia.org/wiki/Cruzadas
- http://www.opus-info.org/index.php?title=Testimonio_de_mi_salida_de_la_Obra
- https://www.google.com/search?q=guerra+en+francia+1940&tbm=isch&source=iu&ictx=1&fir=NdfppWG5IbWdfM%253A%252Cxu3BF5LsYJD0hM%252C%252Fm%252F01h6pn&vet=1&usg=AI4_-kQZAUKmsKYZwlTfdaYj6Zslj-

ihdw&sa=X&ved=2ahUKEwjRrvbSiN3jAhUGAXwKHYkvDMIQ_B0wHXoECAYQAw#imgrc=NdfppWG5IbWdfM:

- https://www.laizquierdadiario.com.bo/La-Iglesia-catolica-y-su-persecucion-a-las-mujeres
- https://es.wikipedia.org/wiki/Caza_de_brujas
- https://www.20minutos.es/noticia/357746/0/iglesia/dinero/anticonceptivos/
- https://www.google.com/search?q=aspergers&rlz=1C1JZAP_enUS860US860&oq=aspergers&aqs=chrome..69i57j0l5.7266j0j7&sourceid=chrome&ie=UTF-8
- https://www.netflix.com/title/80122179
- https://www.laizquierdadiario.com/El-imperio-britanico-la-iglesia-catolica-y-la-triste-realidad-de-los-ninos-migrantes
- https://www.bbc.com/mundo/noticias-internacional-39105765
- https://www.netflix.com/us-es/title/80991879
- https://diariocorreo.pe/mundo/australia-religiosa-pide-perdon-por-abusos-sexuales-en-orfanato-581809/
- https://elpais.com/diario/1997/06/11/sociedad/865980004_850215.amp.html
- https://www.netflix.com/title/80098103?s=i&trkid=13752289
- https://es.wikipedia.org/wiki/Philomena
- https://en.wikipedia.org/wiki/Philomena_Lee

- https://es.m.wikipedia.org/wiki/Oranges_and_Sunshine
- https://es.wikipedia.org/wiki/Spotlight
- https://www.netflix.com/title/80063867?s=i&trkid=13630398

ABOUT THE AUTHOR

HELENA PANEYKO is the result of the combination of nationalities and cultures. She handles every challenge she sets for herself with intensity and tenacity. Helena was born and raised in Venezuela, where she also received her veterinarian's degree. Her talent for leadership made her President of the Student Council of the Veterinarian Faculty (UCV) and later on gave her the opportunity to serve as a Deputy in the Venezuelan National Congress. She also conducted her own radio show and was a long-time collaborator for Estampas magazine.

In 1997, she emigrated to the USA along with her children, Alejandro and Daniela. In the United States, she continued her formal education earning a Master's in Education (Management and Leadership). She has lived in a number of countries, including Spain and Ireland.

In 2015 she decided to follow the pilgrimage of Santiago de Compostela from Lisbon in what she considers one of her most gratifying life experiences... so far.

As a writer, she has won the Rainshadow Poetry Competition in Sequim, WA, and her work has been published in the competition's anthology.

She has also successfully published her first two short story books, "IMPOSIBLE" and "HALF AND HALF." In these books she bares her soul and expresses her most profound reflections in her characteristically creative and original manner.

Her short stories were selected and published in the compilation "IN THE WORDS OF OLYMPIC PENINSULA AUTHORS," Volume 2.

This new publication is her first short novel, a story filled with passion and protest based on fictionalized realities, stories known by many but concealed by all.

Helena continues on her path as a rising figure in the literary world.

A FEW THOUGHTS FROM THE AUTHOR

This is a novel about discoveries, transformations, secrets, and taboos that we all know exist, but few wish to openly talk about. On the one side there are those who need to overcome ingrained shame and survivor's guilt. Then there is the incredibly powerful Church that, to this day, still acts selfishly, instilling fear and threats of retribution.

I have devoted years to investigating the stories that I write about in this book.

The few brave ones, the ones who were determined to share their stories despite all odds, were the ones who experienced the scenarios you are about to see unfold in this novel.

Words cannot express the feelings of those who were preyed upon. They were forced to internalize unimaginable disillusionment and frustration. For this reason I would like to use my words to express the deepest sympathy, understanding, and apologies.

As difficult as it may be to accept many of these seemingly fictitious stories, many of the stories are in fact true. For this reason and to protect my sources, names and details have, of course, been changed.

I reprehend the abuse of power by political, religious, financial, military, or any other authorities. This power should never be used to exert manipulative practices one way or another.

I reprehend the hypocrisy of "*mea culpa*" and public displays of repentance that run contrary to the most fundamental rules of coexistence.

Guilt, fear, shame…

I am curious to know who the culprits confess to. Who gets to hear their secret stories? Who absolves them of all their sins?

I would like to encourage those who are not sure about their origins to find the courage to dig deeper, find their truth, and claim justice and admittance of responsibility for what they went through. This especially applies to the sons and daughters of priests and nuns who never got to know their real parents and were systematically lied to.

I seek justice for those who are unable to challenge the untruth themselves. I want to use my voice to yell this all out for those who think they have no voice, those who were taught to fear and remain silent.

I must confess that what started as an attempt to write a novel existing between fiction and reality, eventually became a fascinating research project (with ramifications) that far exceeded my original vision.

I have included a bibliography with some of the sources I have relied on for this novel. Again, the stories I base this novel on are real and cruel stories that I feel should not remain ignored.

My main message is that life should never be obscurantism. On the contrary, life is light and an infinite gift and it should be that way for everyone.

When I started writing this novel, I had no idea where it would take me. Whenever I sat in front of my computer I felt as though my fingers started typing without even being asked to do so. Every page I wrote seemed to burst with questions I tried to answer. To a certain extent, it became my personal duty to fulfill this self-imposed task.

I would like to clarify that not everyone is guilty and that I am not trying to be a judge, but many minds can and do inflict a great deal of damage. So far, they have been protected by their Superiors, by Drug Trafficking Cartels, Heads of State, Dictators, Guerrillas, as well as unscrupulous Money Launderers whose profits, guarded by the authorities and religious syndicates operating with absolute impunity, remain safe at the Vatican Bank.

The stories I narrate have historical roots that we carry collectively and which are related to religious scandals: celibacy, instituted during the two Letran Councils of 1123 and 1139 and based on the fear of *"moral degradation"* of the clergy, the Crusades, pitting Catholic and Muslim powers against each other just before the discovery of the Americas and encouraged by the corresponding Pope, and the looting of gold and women from the indigenous American peoples starting in 1492. Many atrocities were justified in the name of God. I may also add to this very preliminary list the well-known practices of witch-hunting and burning as well as the indiscriminate persecution of women.

The pederasty scandals, the Vatican-sponsored hypocritical partnerships with big pharmaceutical companies producing male enhancers and contraceptives and its political alliances designed to retain control over the people...

In addition to all these transgressions and not well known to the rest of the world is the practice of labor and sexual slavery, which is also documented in this work.

I ask, is there any kind of public *"Religious Impeachment"* that could be implemented under the Law? Could some of the abuses be considered as violation of Human Rights? And if so, why don't we see more of it? And if not, is it not about time, or better, overdue?

This literary experience has been like a bottomless Pandora's Box with many surprises... and the more information I gathered, the more I discovered. I am sure I will fall short in the end.

The characters, some real and others fictitious, belong to a multicultural and hybrid family. They all have different dreams, inclinations, and expectations. Faced with their own challenges, they discover that their lives are a maze of many crossroads and mirrors filled with secrets, frustrations, as well as a deep fear of expressing themselves, of questioning and confronting their own truths, of being punished, of going against the precepts set by their parents, their teachers, and those who dared to be their confessors and mentors. At the same time, however, they also discover that life is filled with hope, will, and passion.

It is very important to me at this point to honor my belief in the Universal Creator.

Made in the USA
Columbia, SC
09 March 2024

32363799R00052